HIND POCKET BOOKS

COWS DON'T FLY!

Dr. Promod Batra (1936-2016) was born on 15 October 1936 in Sargodha a city in the Punjab Province located in modern day Pakistan. He was the eldest of five children and his father was an officer with the railways. As a child he was not exceptionally meritorious academically, but was blessed with the talent to learning on his own, think and find simple answers to questions on life. A habit which became his passion and then gave birth to his company – Think Inc.

PROMOD BATRA

COWS DON'T FLY!

Thank God!

HIND POCKET BOOKS
An imprint of Penguin Random House

HIND POCKET BOOKS

USA | Canada | UK | Ireland | Australia
New Zealand | India | South Africa | China | Singapore

Hind Pocket Books is part of the Penguin Random House group of companies whose addresses can be found at www.hindpocketbooks.com

Published by Hind Pocket Books Pvt. Ltd
4th Floor, Capital Tower 1, MG Road,
Gurugram 122 002, Haryana, India

Penguin Random House India

First published in Hind Pocket Books by Penguin Random House India 2019
This edition published in 2022

10 9 8 7 6 5 4 3 2

ISBN 9789353494186

Printed at Repro India Limited

www.penguin.co.in

FSC www.fsc.org MIX Paper from responsible sources FSC® C047271

This is a legitimate digitally printed version of the book and therefore might not have certain extra finishing on the cover.

Contents

Introduction

“Buddy! A bird in the sky dropped its shit in my eye, I do not worry, I do not cry. I am just happy that cows do not fly”.

The attitude of a person measures the altitude of his success. The world is viewed differently by everyone, and it is an individual's perception that governs his ambition and the way he views the opportunities in this world. It is entirely your prerogative whether you want to be a mournful *Dukhiram* for whom life passes by as a series of distressing events or a cheerful *Sukhiram* who believes in taking the ups and downs of life in his stride, with a smile on his face and positive thoughts in his mind.

The problem most people have is that they believe that happiness and success come from outside of them. Many were never taught to live with positive intention and be driven by inspired action...their own! To further compound matters, we see life working for others around us and often times wonder or ask, "Why them and not me?" Instead, we should be asking ourselves, "Why not me?"

And all this is possible through a change in attitude for the positive. I learnt this lesson when I was in America. After completing my B.Com from Shri Ram College of Commerce, I went to the University of Minnesota for my M.B.A. In the U.S., my first years were full of challenges and it was there when I started learning from practical experiences of life. Slowly I became a keen observer. I started collecting wisdoms of everyday life through aphorisms and motivational stories.

My life at Escorts was really a college of practical learning. There I faced many ups and downs, but I never went into sulk, rather I did my job more efficiently. I worked there for 33 years and retired happily.

Then started my tryst with the writing of management and motivational books. The journey is very long and enjoying. I have authored over 50 books, all received very well by the readers.

In this book, you will find some very inspirational short stories, full of wisdom of everyday life. I have acquired them from here and there, polished them and fine-tuned these for you. Much of that is written here is based on my own experiences and the philosophy which I have developed for myself by active interaction with others as well as a study of the writings and experiences of great leaders of Indian mythology, in addition to men and women in flesh and blood who lived not too long ago or are still alive and vibrant.

There is a mega-dose of common sense in what is written in these stories, which can be translated into practice. You too can adapt these wisdoms to suit your requirements. Still better, you can add to them your own ideas and experiences to make your life more successful and happy.

Remember, that while we can moan about misfortunes that befall us, we must also celebrate that *Cows don't Fly!* – otherwise they would shower us with blessings! Happy reading!

Promod Batra

February 2014, New Delhi

Remember any good work ever done by us never goes in vain. It comes back to us suitably rewarded in any form.

1

Once More, makes All the Difference, Many Times!

Man has a hidden treasure within. Difficulties and setbacks bring it forth.

Two frogs fell into a shallow well. And their friends started shouting instructions! Do this and do that. After a while, the frogs outside the well realised that it was a hopeless case. And they suggested to them to give up and await their death! One frog accepted his fate and did nothing. But the other frog kept on jumping. The frogs outside the well started shouting again and again and gesturing to the second frog to give up. After a while, the second frog gave himself a big push and he managed finally to jump out of the well.

There was a lot of excitement and happiness. The frogs asked the second frog why he kept on jumping, when they were shouting instructions to give up! And the second frog proudly replied, "I am deaf! I did not hear you but it looked as if you were encouraging me."

Friends, listen to many people and every opinion but do what you think you can do! Become a "can do person".

A challenge is a part of life – take it in your stride knowing that you will win most of the time, lose some of the time, but become a better man either way for having tried.

2

What Will People Say...

What will my friends say?
What will my colleagues say?
What will my neighbour say?
These are immobilising thoughts.
Remember the story of the father, son and donkey going to the market. They got so influenced by what people thought of them that neither could ride the donkey.

There was a man in this world, who has become a "lighthouse" for millions of stressful people who followed him. His name was Abraham Lincoln. His resume is as follows:

- Age 22, failed in business.
- Age 23, ran for legislature and was defeated.
- Age 24, failed again in business.
- Age 25, elected to legislature.
- Age 26, sweetheart died.
- Age 27, had a nervous breakdown.
- Age 29, defeated for speaker.
- Age 31, defeated for elector.
- Age 34, defeated for Congress.
- Age 37, elected to Congress.
- Age 39, defeated for Congress.
- Age 46, defeated for Senate.
- Age 47, defeated for Vice President.
- Age 49, defeated for Senate
- Age 51, elected President of the United State of America.

Abraham Lincoln did not bother what people said about him when he failed. Even when he became the President, people still criticised him, but instead of becoming stressful, he expressed this deathless line: "No man is good enough to be President, but someone has to be."

3

Make Your Family Your Priority No. 1

You are your children's hero. Remember that. Also remember that God has fitted the world's largest and best video tape recorders in your children's mind. The way you treat your parents, employees, associates, customers; well, it is all getting taped to be played back to you later!

Once, a Professor displayed certain materials on his table. When the class began, wordlessly he picked up a very large glass jug and filled it with rocks, about 2 inches in diameter.

He then asked the students whether the jug was full. They agreed that it was. The Professor then picked up some of the pebbles and put them into the jug. He shook the jug lightly. The pebbles, of course, rolled into the open areas between the bigger rocks. He then asked the students again whether the jug was full. They agreed it was. The Professor picked up some sand and poured it into the jug. Of course, the sand filled up the jug. He then asked once more whether the jug was full. The students responded with yes.

The Professor then poured two cans of beer into the jug effectively filling the empty space between the sand. The students laughed. As soon as the laughter subsided, the Professor continued, "I want you to recognize that this jug represents your life. The rocks are the important things – in your life – your family, your partner, your health, and your children, things that if everything else was lost and only they remained, your life would still be almost full. The pebbles are the other things that matter like your job, your house, your car. The sand is everything else – the small stuff. If you put the sand into the jug first, there is no room for the pebbles or rocks. The same goes for your life. If you spend all your time and energy on the small stuff, you will never have room for the things that are important for you."

Pay attention to the things that are critical to your happiness. Play with your children. Take time to get medical checkups. Take your partner out. There will always be time to go to work, clean the house, give a dinner party. Take care of the rocks first – the things that really matter. Set your priorities. The rest is just sand.

One of the students raised her hand and inquired what the beer represented. The Professor smiled and said, "I'm glad you asked. It just goes to show you that no matter how full your life may seem, there's always room for a couple of beers!"

4

Do, Do, Do...
Try, Try, Try...
Get Busy!

If I had 8 hours
to chop a tree
I would spend
6 hours sharpening
my axe.

Two boys were walking down a country road when they saw two milk cans being loaded for delivery to a nearby city. Seeing no one, the boys lifted off the cover of Can Number 1 and dropped in a big bullfrog. Then they lifted off the cover of Can Number 2 and dropped in another bullfrog. Later the cans were picked up and loaded for city delivery.

During the journey, the bullfrog in Can Number 1 said: "This is terrible! I can't lift off the cover of the can because it's too heavy. I have never had a milk bath before, and I can't reach the bottom of the can to get enough pressure to lift the cover, so, what's the use..."– and he gave up trying and quit! When the cover of Can Number 1 was taken off, there was a big dead bullfrog.

The same conditions existed in Can Number 2 and the frog said to himself: "Well, I can't lift off the cover because it's too tight and too heavy, I haven't got a brace and bit to drill a hole to save myself, but, there is one thing I learned to do in liquids and that is to swim."

So, he swam, and swam, and swam, and churned a lump of butter and sat on it. And when the cover was lifted off, out he jumped.

The winner never quits and the quitter never wins! The quitter becomes stressful.

Catch people
doing something
right.

5

Manage Your Anger Creatively and Innovatively!

One weak link can spell disaster for the whole chain. Hence, analyse yourself. See if you have any flaws and frailties that can play havoc with your organisation and your aims.

If you do have an Achilles heel somewhere, attend to it. Remove the weakness. And stride ahead from strength to strength.

Let me give you the famous example of anger from Ramayana. The Ravana was the wisest of the wise, with ten wise heads on his shoulders. However, his success had killed his humility and, along with it, many of his virtues too.

So when his sister Suparnakha, who had her nose chopped off because of her wrongdoing, presented her distorted story, Ravana, who by now had developed the habit of being short tempered, forgot to ask simple questions like:

- Why did you go to meet Ram and Laxman?
- What exactly happened?
- Why shouldn't I talk to Ram and find out his side of the story?

The result was nothing but stress for himself and all his family members. Ravana must have been the most stressful person who ever lived in India – all because of his habit of being short tempered!

So, my friends, why not think and reflect, and engage in frequent self-audits to reduce your anger and decide what you want to be – Ram or Ravana.

It is sure that everything in future is not going to happen, as you want. Some adverse things are inevitable in future not only for you but also with everybody because life is like that, a mixture of pleasure and pain.

6

Do Your Networking Now!

The firmest friendships
have been formed in
mutual adversity,
as iron is most
strongly united by the
fiercest flames.

The Crow is a very proactive bird, beautiful and handsome – depends upon how you look at it! Graceful black and grey – black is beautiful! A crow is very smart and has a tremendous instinct for survival.

May we suggest you to do this experiment? Take some food and spread it around on the ground. Wait for a couple of minutes and you will find a crow appearing from nowhere. When the crow finds plenty of food, it will start cawing and soon you may have a few crows having a feast at your expense! A simple pleasure of life! We know a crow is a thinking bird (remember the "crow, pitcher of water and stones" story).

A crow understands fully that when he invites other crows to share his "food find", others will reciprocate in a similar situation!

In management, it is called "NETWORKING".

- When a crow finds food, it calls out for other crows and shares the food.
- What do we do when we get some information? Hoard it or share it? Become a Crow!

Compensation is a right, recognition is a gift.

7

Forgiveness is the Key to form Good Friendships!

Friendship improves happiness, and abates misery, by doubling our joy, and dividing our grief.

Two friends were walking through the desert. During some point of the journey, they had an argument, and one friend slapped the other in the face. The one who got slapped was hurt, but without saying anything, wrote in the sand: *"Today my best friend slapped me in the face."*

They kept on walking until they found an oasis, where they decided to take a bath. The one who was slapped got stuck in the mire and started drowning, but his friend saved him. After he recovered from the near-drowning, he wrote on a stone: *"Today my best friend saved my life."*

The friend who had slapped and saved his best friend asked him, "After I hurt you, you wrote in the sand and now you write on a stone. Why?" The other friend replied: "When someone hurts us we should write it down in the sand where winds of FORGIVENESS can erase it away but, when someone does something good for us, we must engrave it in stone where no wind can ever erase it."

We shall learn to write our hurts in the sand and carve our benefits on stone.

It is said that it takes a minute to find a special person, an hour to appreciate him, a day to love him, but then an entire life to enjoy.

It's not great ideas
that SUCCEED;
its great people
who make them
succeed.

8

Develop an Attitude that a Big Bad Debt Won't Kill You!

The ultimate measure of
a man is not where he
stands in moments of
comfort and convenience,
but where he stands at
times of challenge and
controversy.

– Martin Luther King

Recently at a party I met a big wholesaler of books, Om Arora, who is well established in the export trade. He had invited all his contacts from all over the world for an annual sales conference. I was introduced to his US importer, one Roger Ericson, and pleasantries were exchanged. I was surprised, because earlier I had met David Massey.

After a while, I asked Om what happened to David and was told that he went belly up, which happened fairly often in the USA. I asked Om if he had lost any money, and he coolly replied, "Only Rs. 6 lacs!"

"How is it that you are so cheerful in spite of this?" I exclaimed. Then Om said the most wonderful thing, which I want to share with you. He said, "I feel happy because in spite of this loss, my business is doing well, and that can only mean that I have become a big businessman. I thank God and pray that he will keep me this way." Amen.

Now, Om is Ganesha while many in his place would have become Gobarganesha!

Before any discussion or argument with a person, you must think whether spending so much time and energy with this person is really of any use or you are just satisfying your false ego.

9

Enjoy the Role of Excellence in Whatever You Do

Ralph Waldo Emerson rightly said: "An institution is the lengthend shadow of one man." History shows whenever a leader has achieved more than ordinary successes, he has gathered his team first. Of course, you have to inspire them, set course, provide the momentum and steer them in profitable directions.

I had flown in to Dallas for the sole purpose of calling on a client. Time was of the essence and my plan induced a quick turnaround trip from and back to the airport. A spotless cab pulled up. The driver rushed to open the passenger door for me and made sure I was comfortably seated before he closed the door. As he got in the driver's seat, he mentioned that the neatly folded Wall Street Journal next to me was for my use. He then showed me several tapes and asked me what type of music I would enjoy.

Well! I looked around for a "Candid Camera!" Wouldn't you? I could not believe the service I was receiving! I took the opportunity to say, "Obviously you take great pride in your work. You must have a story to tell."

"You bet," he replied, "I used to be in Corporate America. But I got tired of thinking my best would never be good enough. I decided to find my niche in life where I could feel proud of being the best I could be. I knew I would never be a rocket scientist, but I love driving cars, being of service and feeling like I have done a full day's work and done it well. I evaluated my personal assets and... wham! I became a cab driver. One thing I know for sure, to be good in my business I could simply just meet the expectations of my passengers. But to be GREAT in my business, I have to EXCEED the customer's expectations. I like both the sound and the return of being 'great' better than just getting by on 'average'"

Did I tip him big time? You bet! Corporate America's loss is the travelling folk's friend!

10

Sharpen your Mental Axe!

Excellence means doing the little things well – doing a thousand things one per cent better rather than doing one thing a thousand per cent better.

Once upon a time, a very strong woodcutter asked for a job from a timber merchant, and he got it. The pay was really good and so were the working conditions. For that reason, the woodcutter was determined to do his best.

His boss gave him an axe and showed him the area where he was supposed to work.

The first day, the woodcutter brought 18 trees.

"Congratulations," the boss said. "Go on that way!"

Very motivated for the boss's words, the woodcutter tried harder the next day, but he only could bring only 15 trees.

The third day he tried even harder, but he only could bring 10 trees. Day after day he was bringing less and less trees.

"I must be losing strength," the woodcutter thought. He went to the boss and apologized, saying that he could not understand what was going on.

"When was the last time you sharpened your axe?" the boss asked.

"Sharpen? I had no time to sharpen my axe. I have been very busy trying to cut trees..."

Treat your people like your customers

11

The Importance of Right Feedback

Salesman normally do not listen. They get a wrong notion that they must keep on talking and talking, whether the prospects is listening or not. Listen and hear what the prospect says.

Every company and every individual would like to know how they are doing. Normally, companies send out questionnaires or check their sales records or balance sheets. When such questionnaires are sent out, a few are filled in, for the most part very casually.

Years ago, my friend and guru, Mr. Mehta, told me about an experience with an international airline.

Once, on a long flight, when he had finished his meal and was relaxing, an air hostess came and sat next to him. She started asking him innocent questions about the airline and its services. Mr. Mehta asked why the airline didn't give out questionnaires to be filled in. She replied that the airline's attitude was to find the truth in a qualitative manner. This way, she said, though they got fewer responses, they were the best to help them meet their goal of providing the best service to their customers.

To most of us, life is statistics and numbers. We measure our success by sales figures, market sales, market value, etc. In the process, we lose out on the "soul" of life. To really find out how we are doing, we need direct, qualitative feedback.

To get the truth, think about your attitudes. You

will be walking that much faster, with more sparkle in your eyes, more life in your heart and more peace in your soul. Amen!

12

Take Time to Make a Critical Decision

Achieving goals
should be a
pleasure, not
a worrisome
journey!

On learning about the death of his son, Abhimanyu, at the hands of Sindhunaresh by foul means, Arjuna takes an oath to kill him before the sunset the next day or commit suicide. Well, it sounds good, but his guru and friend, Krishna, gives him a good verbal thrashing the next day during the battle. Arjuna is anxious to achieve his goal and is doing his best, but his one eye is on the sun's position in the sky!

In Mahabharata, Arjuna has been shown to have a confused mind. But he is intelligent enough to have a good consultant friend, Lord Krishna.

Without Krishna, Arjuna may not have started the Kurukshetra war. Without him, he may not have killed Sindhunaresh, if Krishna had not played the tricks of temporarily hiding the sun.

Krishna tells Arjuna, (and this is pregnant with good learning lessons for us as managers:) "...What was the need to set such a stupid deadline to achieve your goal? Now, instead of focusing on your goal with clear vision, there is 'dust' in your eyes (i.e. the setting sun)."

Arjuna listens and thinks about Krishna's forceful discourse and says sorry several times.

Deadlines are the ultimate triggers for inspiration and perspiration to work hard, but if in the process you kill yourself or others working with you, it is not the right thing to do. Achieving goals should be a pleasure. It should be a journey, which you should enjoy and not rush through as if the journey is a drudgery.

Think about it. That is it, buddy!

13

Make Good Friends Before You Need Them

Never develop a friendship with a man who is not better than yourself.

Visualise the Mahabharata at Kurukshetra. The Chariot, Krishna as the Divine Charioteer, ready to listen to his friend's directions. And Arjuna, seeing the great Kauravas (Bhisma, Dronacharya, Karna...), suddenly gets the Arjuna-disease!"

Arjuna starts weakening. He starts mentally manufacturing cowardly thoughts of retreat from the post of duty where destiny has called upon him to act: Fighting is Arjuna's karma.

Krishna listens to Arjuna and is silent as a statue. Arjuna appeals to him not to start the battle. Krishna listens. Krishna is silent. Arjuna goes on and on with his long-drawn-out limping arguments.

Let us draw an inspiration from his famous battle scene. In our day-to-day life at the office and at home, whenever we see difficulties ahead we come up with several mental scenes. We find excuses. Moods. Visions. Cant's. We get into our cocoon, our shell, our box! The womb mentality!

What to do? Listen. Listen. Listen to yourself, in yourself, in your mind. The right part of your mind is shouting at the left part to do your karma. Many of us have the tendency, the temptation to switch off! It's simple. But then our right mind, our karma, starts shouting louder and louder. This is the Mahabharata. Don't bully that voice! Listen. Try. Act. You will be on the path of a karmayogi. You will start thinking outside your box.

14

Use the Concept of Sense of Approximation

A person who uses his imagination creatively may do better than a person with more resources of men, money and materials.

One morning, Akbar asked his Navratnas, "How many crows are there in all of Agra? It is important that we have this information immediately. And you have to give me the correct answer, or else there will be serious trouble, I warn you."

The Navratnas were scared. Nobody knew the number of crows in the city. The Navratnas were in a fix. If they did not answer the king they would be punished, and if they give the wrong number, then too, they would be punished.

Only Raja Birbal was calm. After some time he said, "Your Majesty, there are exactly ten thousand, six hundred and sixty six crows in all of Agra."

"Are you sure, Birbal?" asked the emperor. "We shall have the crows counted to make sure the number you have said is correct".

"By all means. Your Majesty," said Birbal, calmly. "But I cannot be sure that all the crows will remain in Agra till the counting is complete. Many may go and visit their friends and relations in Delhi, in which case there will be less than the number I give you. It is also possible that many relatives and friends of these crows may come to visit them in Agra, and so it will increase the number. But I can surely say that at this moment there are ten thousand, six hundred and sixty six crows in Agra".

The king burst out laughing and said, "Birbal, you are amazing!"

15

Honesty is Still the Best Policy

Honesty is still the best policy, with a little bit of common sense.

Once a general manager wanted to test his people who had come from all over India about their values of life.

He announced that in their seminar folder, there is a PVC pouch and in it there is a seed. When they return, they must put it in a good soil in a pot and look after it very well. He would hold a competition in the next year's seminar and then the best plants would be awarded suitably.

Everyone did what was told to him. A year passed quickly. And next year in a big hall, there were hundreds of pots and a great variety of plants – really a great scene. Except one pot in which the soil was there and no plant! The owner was standing quietly and seemingly ashamed of himself!

The general manager called him on the stage. He asked him what happened and he told him the truth. He planted the seed which he was given – and did whatever was to be done – but nothing happened!

The general manager declared him the winner! Everyone was shocked. It was announced, "Gentleman, the seeds I gave you were boiled seeds. You planted them and nothing happened! You acted smartly and used some other seeds. This man was honest to his work and, therefore, he did not cheat me or himself!"

Your mind is a Thoughts Factory, and you are the production manager. It can produce either positive or negative thoughts. The ideas of others are your raw materials.

16

Learn to Love What You Do for a Living

There is nobody in the worldwho knows nothing and there is nobody in the world who knows everything. Everybody knows something, which you don't know. Learn from everybody.

Choose a job you love. And, you will never have to work a day in your life!

A few decades ago, while doing my MBA, I worked as a part time Animal Research Lab Attendant at the University of Minnesota Hospital in their Surgery Department. I was looking after 60 dogs on whose hearts doctors from all over America were working.

The doctors, working more or less round the clock, had ear-to-ear smiles on their faces, a song in their hearts and happiness oozing out of their cheeks. They were actually getting less money than some of the skilled technicians in the laboratory who were more often bitching and complaining about the working conditions even though they worked from 8 to 5 with long breaks for lunch and coffee!

In the beginning, it was somewhat puzzling, but quite soon I learnt a lesson from this strange phenomenon: The doctors were doing what they loved to do, while the technicians were doing what they had to do.

During these hours, the technicians had heartburns, but the doctors rejoiced in even small achievements. Good for the doctors' hearts, is it not?

More easily said than done. Agreed. Many people do not like what they are doing, but they can still reduce their stress considerably if they follow the principles of profitable heart management.

17

Slow and Steady Still Wins the Race

Follow no one
but learn from
everywhere.

Here is a very good story told by Mr. M.A. Hakeem, Secretary General, SCOPE, about the "slow-working, sleepy" Japanese.

A six-member Japanese delegation went to Texas to buy cows. The American farmer showed them the works, and told the Japanese that he will offer them a good deal. And it was that, if the Japanese selects the cows, each cow is for $100 and if the American selects the cow the price would be $90. Well, the American expected a quick decision, a decision on the spot like we Indians and Americans do.

But the Japanese believe that slow and steady wins the race. They excused themselves to a meeting room for an hour. The American was going crazy, cursing the Japanese as slow thinkers.

Finally when the Japanese emerged, he anxiously asked about their decision. The Japanese member quietly said in his slow and broken English, "Mr. Bill, we would like you to select the cows for us."

American, "How many"

Japanese, "All".

The sleepy Japanese got the deal, and the smart American sold all, at a loss!

Your life on the earth would be considered worth only when you can give to the world more than what you have got from it.

18

Show Respect to Your Little Customer to Teach Your Employees

Present customers are and will continue to be the best prospects for more business! Spend time and effort to read your present customers accurately, tune in to what they require in terms of assistance and support. Do not take them for granted.

In Osaka, there was a very famous sweet shop. The shop was known for the fine sweets it sold. The very rich patronized the shop, for the prices were very high. The shop owner always stayed at the back of the shop and very seldom came out to attend to the customers, no matter how rich.

One day, a very poor man walked in to the shop; his clothes were torn and his hair unkempt. The poor man reluctantly and deliberately approached the counter. Before the poor man could reach the counter, the shop owner darted from the back room, pushed aside his sales person and then with great enthusiasm greeted the poor man and patiently waited for the poor man to gather all his pocket change to pay for one piece of sweet.

The shop owner very courteously handed the poor man the piece of sweet and while the poor man was leaving, the shop owner kept bowing in reverence.

When the poor customer left, the salesman could not resist asking the shop owner why he had personally attended to the poor man when he never bothered to come out when rich customers came to buy sweets.

The shop owner replied, "The poor man really

honoured us by spending all the money he had to buy one piece of sweet.

He will really savour our sweet. To the rich our sweets taste good but are not as valuable as to the poor man."

19

Manufacture an Attitude of *KFP*

The pessimist complains about the wind; the optimist expects it to change; the realist adjusts the cell.

Manufacture an attitude of *KFP – Kee Pharak Painda* (What difference does it make) – after all everything in life is not a question of life and death.

I failed in 9th class and my brother passed! (We were both in the same class!!) My father was upset for a minute or two and then responded, "...son, *kee pharak painda,* you worked hard, you failed. Next year, I am sure, you will do well..."

My father was a very wise person. He did not insult me by usual dialogues that fathers blurt out, being in the state of Dukhi Ram.

By this response, he made me a little more tough to face adversities in life. Similarly, during my 33 years in Escorts, my seven bosses did not give me many promotions or increments.

It used to hurt a little... but the attitude always was... KFP! Also the thought "It ain't over, till it is over!" I diverted my attitude towards sharing my collection of ideas and experiences with my professional colleagues, dealers and friends.

Result: at 66,1 have got over fifty publications to my credit which give me lots of money, feeling of success and happiness... feeling of 90:10 (Sukhi Ram 90%; Dukhi Ram 10%)

Pride and arrogance lead to definite downfall of the person. This is a divine law and doesn't spare anyone.

20

Maintain Class and Grace in All Circumstances: It Really Matters

When the man you like switches from what he said a year ago, or four years ago, he is broad-minded person who has courage enough to change his mind with changing conditions. When a man you don't like does it, he is a liar who has broken his promise.

It was my sister Katie's wedding day, and she floated through the reception hall smiling and thanking guests, dancing with each of the grandpas, and taking time to chat with the flower girls.

She looked so beautiful and serene that no one would have guessed that the florist had used the wrong flowers, the 3-tiered cake had arrived lopsided, and a bridesmaid had torn her skirt minutes before the ceremony.

Incidents that could have turned the day into a tense and disappointing event were cause for laughter because of Katie's outlook. Behind the scenes, I watched as she responded calmly and sympathetically to the apologetic florist, and laughed and posed for candid pictures with the uneven cake.

When the bridesmaid tripped in her heels and tore the hem of her skirt, Katie didn't panic, but assisted her in stapling the tear together, which resulted in more candid photos of the two of them posing with the stapler.

While friends discuss their confrontations with stressed brides, I remain silent. I have a picture hanging on my wall of my smiling sister posing with a lopsided cake that reminds me of the lasting impression of class and grace in all circumstances.

The human spirit is nurtured by praise, as much as the soil the water and the sun nurture a seedling.

21

Walk an Extra Mile

Give to the world the best you have and the best will come back to you.

Recently, my buddy Ajay Raman called me up to know the number of our mutual friend Krishna Nagpal, who had left Escorts a decade ago.

I did not have it. But another friend Sudhir Chaudhary, I knew, was his buddy. So I informed Ajay Raman to call Sudhir. Then I changed my mind as I wanted to do a good deed for the day! I called Sudhir who gave me Krishan's number. Immediately, I called Krishnan and said hello and told him Ajay wanted to talk to him.

Then I called Ajay and gave him Krishnan's number. In the process, I talked to my lost friends, felt happy all over.

This action was triggered by something I read somewhere on selling. A customer met his real estate salesman on a road and asked for some information.

The salesman suggested him to call such and such place where the customer can get the information.

A good salesman will never do it. He would tell the customer that he will find out and call him later. And at the first opportunity, he should call the number, get more information than that is required, and with a smile in his voice, brightness in the eyes, chest puffed-up, should call his customer. Then the customer will never go anywhere else. Simple. Is not it?

Look out for opportunities to do good things. Do essentials and cut out inessentials of life. Cut in half, if you have an old habit of reading newspapers cover to cover! Good luck.

22

Do a Self-audit

You get your accounts audited. Do you get yourself audited?

When I was growing up, I heard an interesting story which I want to share with you. It has inspired me a lot, made me think.

There was once a mighty king. In many ways, he was uncertain of his ministers and employees. He did not trust anyone, except a monkey!

One day, the king was very tired as it happened to be very hot and humid. He retired to his chambers and instructed his faithful monkey to ensure that no one disturbed his siesta.

After a while, the king drifted into a sound sleep and there was pin-drop silence. Suddenly, a fly flew in and sat on the magnificent nose of the great king.

The monkey very respectfully shooed it away. After a while, the fly came back and the monkey again sent it away. It kept on and on. While the monkey was getting irritated, the fly was enjoying playing with the magnificent nose of the king.

Suddenly, the monkey had a brilliant idea. He got out the king's finest and sharpest sword. And in a flash, he killed the insolent fly, and also chopped away the magnificent nose!

Moral: Keep your work in perspective and your feet on the ground.

If you do not update your knowledge from books and seminars, you may come to look like this to your boss, your friends and to yourself too!

Reflect on what you are doing. Don't be a "monkey" for your boss.

23

From the Other Side of the River

Marketing is really a form of communication.

During my school days, I used to go on vacation to our native place, a small town on the banks of a river. In the evenings, I normally strolled to the local market to watch the vendors sell their wares. Once, among the vegetable vendors, I spotted a young boy with a basket full of brinjals, sitting alongside other brinjal sellers. I watched him with interest, because he looked so small and helpless beside the other more experienced vendors who were outselling him, by sheer aggressiveness. Our young lad made no sale at all.

For a few days in succession, I saw the youngster sadly walking back home with all his unsold brinjals. Till one fine day, I suddenly heard him shouting.

"Four annas a kilo, brinjals. The best brinjals. Brinjals from the other side of the river: Yes, from the other side..."

And within minutes, he had sold every single brinjal he had. Other brinjals were equally good. His price was not lower either. And yet he had been able to outsell the veterans by making his brinjals "seem" different.

My curiosity got the better of me and I walked up to him to find out how he had managed such a feat.

It transpired that every day when the young boy went home with his unsold brinjals, his father beat him up and called him a "good for nothing". That particular day, the father had given him an ultimatum. If he could not sell the brinjals, he need not take the trouble of crossing the river to reach home and he should remain on this side.

"That is when," said the boy, "it struck me that I and my brinjals belonged to the other side of the river."

24

Father, Son & Donkey... With a New Moral

Any fool can criticise, condemn and complain – and most fools do.

A wise man was exposing his son to the realities of life. His technique was to let his son make his own observations and draw his own conclusions.

One fine morning, at 6 o'clock, the father woke up his son and both of them, with their donkey, started their journey to the market. The donkey was walking silently as donkeys do! On one side of it walked the father and on the other was his son – both lost in their respective noble thoughts.

A few men stopped them and asked why one of them was not riding the donkey. The obedient son insisted that the father should ride, but the father insisted that the son should do so. Finally, the son perched himself on the donkey. After a while, they were stopped again and the people commented: "Is it fair that while the old man is walking, the young man is riding the donkey?" So, the obedient son got down and the father took the seat and they started again on their journey. Again, after a while, they were stopped and the people remarked: "Is it fair for the man to ride while the son is walking?" In all his wisdom, the son also took his seat behind his father.

Well, now it seemed quite alright, but they were

stopped once again. The men quipped, “Look at the heartless father and son and poor donkey!”

The son got confused. He could not think of any other combination among his father, himself and the donkey. He mediated. He realized. Smiling at his father he said, “Father, in my opinion, you ride the donkey because I think it is the right thing to do.” The father felt happy; his son had learnt to think independently.

Moral: Think. Decide. And do what you think is right.

25

A Simple, Solution to Provocations

Keep a low profile when the wind blows strong. We cannot direct the wind... But we can adjust our sails.

A certain person was touring a desert area in a tonga (horse-drawn carriage) when signs of a storm appeared on the horizon. The tonga-driver immediately halted his vehicle and explained to his passenger, "The storms in the area could assume frightening proportions. They are so strong that they can carry away anything, great or small, which comes in their path. All the signs tell us that it is just such a storm which is on its way, so you had better get down from the carriage and try to save yourself."

With the storm almost upon him, the passenger headed for a tree to take shelter behind it's trunk. Seeing this, the driver called out to him, "Never take shelter under a tree. It is very dangerous! The greatest of trees fall to the fury of the storm; there is only one way to save yourself. Lie face down on the ground."

The passenger did as he was told, which was just as well, for when the gale came, its intensity was such that it carried trees and roof-tops in its wake. The tonga-driver and his passenger, however, were unaffected by it as they lay motionless on the ground. When the gale had finally blown itself out, the two men stood up, quite unhurt. The passenger was very glad he had taken the tonga-driver's advice.

The intensity of storm is always greater above ground level. The ground, therefore, never receives its full impact. But tall trees are hit by its full force that is why they are uprooted during storms. The grass, which hardly rises above the ground, in a storm never gets affected by it, the best thing to do is keep well down. This is one of nature's lessons, which shows us the way to avoid the storms of life. The simplest way at such times is to keep a low profile. For example, when someone speaks in provocative terms, put your hands over your ears. When someone throws dirt on the wall of your house wash it off with water. When someone indulges in slogan-shouting against you, engage yourself in praying for him.

26

Look for a Blessing in Disguise

You can complain because roses have thorns, or you can rejoice because thorns have roses.

– ZIGGY

It was early morning at the big airport. The weather was very bad. Passengers were waiting to find out whether their flights would be delayed, or even cancelled.

Ahead of me in the line was a little gray haired lady. Ahead of her was a man, red-eyed and rumpled, who evidently had just flown in from the west coast. He was giving the agent a hard time. His flight had been very rough. He hadn't slept. His plane had been incling over the airport for an hour. There hadn't been enough coffee on board for breakfast; some passengers had to do without. He thought this was disgraceful. He said so loudly.

The agent looked tired himself, but he was patient and polite. He apologized for the weather and for the plane's late arrival.

"But the coffee!" snapped the man irately. "There's no excuse! How do you account for that?"

Before the agent could attempt a reply, the old lady reached out and tapped the man on the shoulder. She said mildly, "Do you mind if I say something to you?"

The man turned, looking surprised.

"Sir," said the old lady, "you have just travelled

across an entire continent in five or six hours. You were lifted above the clouds and drawn here through the skies where you saw the dawn rushing to meet you. You have just experienced a miracle that mankind could only dream about for thousands of years. And you stand there complaining about having no coffee."

There was quite a long pause. Finally, the man said, "Madam, you are quite right. Thanks for setting me straight. It will be a long time before I forget what you just said." And he turned away.

27

A Spoonful of Sugar

The greatest motivational act one person can do for another is to listen.

When the first batch of Parsis from Iran landed on the west coast of Gujarat, their community leader – their Peshwa – went straight to the ruling monarch, Yadav Rana, and requested him to allow them to stay in the state. The Raja uttered not a word in reply, but simply handed the Peshwa a glass full to the brim with milk. This was meant to show him that this state already had its full measure of population and that there was no room for any more people.

The Peshwa did not answer in words either. His response was simply to add a spoonful of sugar to the milk and to return it to the Raja.

This was his way of saying that the Parsis would sweeten their milk and take possession of it. That is to say that their presence would add sweetness to the life of the state. The Raja was pleased with the response and gave them permission to stay.

No matter how bad a person is but every person has some 'good' in him. So learn to appreciate others.

28

Be Creative as a Father Too!

You are your children's hero. Remember that. Also remember that God has fitted the wortd's largest and best video tape recorders in your children's mind. The way you treat your parents, employees, associates, customers; well, it is all getting taped to be played back to you later!

A teenager had just passed his driving test and was eager to drive his father's car. His father agreed. He asked his son to drop him at a place that was some 18 miles from home before he took the car for servicing. The father then wanted his son to pick him up at four in the afternoon so that they could go home together.

The boy dropped his father, took the car to the garage and went to watch a film. Losing track of time, he continued to watch the film till 6 pm.

Afraid his father would scold him for being late and would never give him the car again, the boy collected the car, arrived at the appointed place and said, "Dad I'm sorry, I'm late but it took the mechanic longer than usual to service the car."

"Son, I phoned the garage," his father replied. "The car was ready at 4 pm." The boy looked down. "I'm sorry, but I went to watch a film."

"Son, I'm very angry," replied the father after a moment of thought. "But not with you. I'm angry with myself. Where did I go wrong as a father? Why did you have to lie to me? Take the car home. I will introspect as I walk back."

The boy trailed behind his father, imploring him to sit inside the car. But his father continued walking silently, soul-searching all the way back home. Distraught, the son pledged never to lie to his parents.

Change yourself and the world will change.

29

Walk Your Talk, You Will Then Have Conviction

Men and women want to do a good job, a creative Job, and if they are provided the proper environment they will do so.

Once a mother was very stressful because her son was very fond of sugar – anything sugary: he would help himself to anything sweet several times a day, making his mother stressful. After talking with several friends, she decided to go to a great guru. After offering her courtesies, she told the guru about her big problem. The guru listened attentively and advised them to come after fifteen days.

The mother and son did so, and the guru asked them to come again after twenty days. Again the mother and son did so. Again the guru asked them to come after thirty days. They came again and this time the guru was delighted to see them and had a chat with them. The mother got anxious and asked for the *gurumantra*. The guru instructed the son not to eat sugar and took the latter's commitment. Both the guru and disciple seemed to be relating to each other. The mother could not hide her stress and blurted out, "Guruji, if you had to tell him only this, you could have done so several weeks ago!"

The guru, with his usual calm and serenity, stated, "Ma, how could I? I was also eating a lot of sugar and how could I ask him to stop? Now that I have myself done it – given up eating sugar, I can instruct him to do so." Both the mother and son left the ashram with due reverence.

Employees will never treat customers any better than they are being treated.

30

Manage Your *Suparnakhas!*

People are seldom angry for the reason they think they are angry. There is usually something else at the bottom of it.

Do you have a "Suparnakha" in your business? I used to watch the Ramayana episodes on TV every Sunday with my "third-eye" open with a view to share my inspirational thoughts with you that may bring more profit and happiness.

Suparnakha, in Ravana's Darbar, pleaded for revenge – Laxman having cut her nose. Ravana – a very, very learned man – sensibly asked her, "What happened?" Suparnakha, in her superbly cunning way replied emotionally, "Brother, while wandering in the forest, I saw Ram and Laxman with a beautiful lady. I wanted to bring that charming lady as a gift for you."

Ravana, the wisest of men, for reasons well known to him, without seeing through his third eye, believed his sister and went in for a fight which resulted in his complete ruin. Now, this is history. But this piece of history (or mythology) can teach us a good lesson.

There are "Suparnakhas" everywhere – among your employees, your friends, your business associates, and so on. Use your "third eye" (God has given third eye in our minds – to everyone) not to destroy but for "Divya Drishti". Try to see through the other person's angle – be it your wife, son, daughter, best employee, best customer

– and use the third principle of management, i.e., Ask! Ask short, short questions using the first principle of management i.e., THINK. Now, if Ravana had only answered his sister Suparnakha: "Sister, thank you for telling me your side of the story. I am very, very sorry to hear it. Tell me more details about it. I will help you and avenge the insult. Sister, I will then send my reps to Ram and Laxman to find out their side of the story and to find out what gains they are expecting by making a move to fight me. Sister, on hearing both the sides, I will draw my action plan; I will use the basic principles of management."

Therefore, always **Think, Ask** and then **Do**. It will help you save many of your "fights" in your business and in your family.

31

Respond to Situations, Don't React!

You can't change anyone. You can't change your father; your mother, your wife, your sister – not even your boss. Change yourself first.

Everybody knew that Akbar was very fond of his grandson. One morning, when Akbar was getting ready for the court, his grandson came running to him. "Grandfather, there is something black in your moustache. Bend down and I will take it out," said his grandson.

As Akbar bent down, his grandson pulled out a hair from his mustache. "Ouch!" screamed Akbar. "Why did you do such naughty thing?" "Ha! Ha! Fooled you!" said his grandson.

"Now go and play, I have to go to the court," Akbar said. On his way to the court, Akbar thought that he would give all his ministers a problem to solve. When he reached the court, he addressed his ministers saying, "Someone pulled a hair from my mustache this morning. I want him to be punished. What punishment should I give him?"

The ministers were shocked when they heard this. "How could anybody dare to pull a hair from the emperor's mustache?" they thought. All the ministers started giving their suggestions.

"The man should be flogged a thousand times," said one courtier.

"He should be imprisoned for life," said somebody:

"The guilty person should be given a kiss," said Birbal.

Everybody was shocked. They thought that Birbal had gone crazy.

"Birbal, can you explain why you suggested such a strange punishment?" asked Akbar.

"Your Majesty, only a child can do such a mischief, and that child could be your grandson," said Birbal.

Akbar and all the courtiers were full of praise for Birbal's cleverness.

32

Speak Softly But Carry A Big Stick!

Kindness is a language we can all speak.
Even the deaf can HEAR it and the BLIND can see.

Dhyan Singh was an apple picker in an orchard at Simla. Life was very peaceful for him... until the management's announcement about a "Zero Defect" programme.

According to the new announcement, each worker was required to sign an undertaking which stated that he would pick only "quality" apples. Obviously an experienced worker like Dhyan Singh could not digest such a rude shock. He told his foreman point blank that he wouldn't sign.

When asked why, he explained that he had been around for a good 30 years in that orchard and he had picked only quality apples. Hence, the Zero Defect gimmick wouldn't work him.

The poor foreman went to the manager. But alas, even the manager, in spite of his best human relations skills, failed miserably in convincing Dhyan Singh. Now the matter went to the proprietor of the orchard, Thakur Devender Singh. The Thakur Saab called Dhyan Singh to his office.

He was not a man who believed in wasting words. In his booming voice he asked, "Dhyan Singh, how long have you been working here?"

Dhyan Singh replied, "Thirty years, Saab."

"Your wife?"

"She is also working for the past 20 years, Saab."

"And your son?"

"He has joined last year and he is working very hard, Saab."

Dhyan Singh was getting very uneasy, while the Thakur Saab took his time to refill his pipe. Dhyan Singh watched him light and blow the smoke.

From somewhere behind the smoke screen, he heard the ominous sounding words being delivered: "Dhyan Singh, if you don't sign, then you all don't work here anymore."

Dhyan Singh didn't think twice. He signed the undertaking on the spot. The Thakur asked him why he had refused earlier. Pat came the reply from Dhyan Singh – "Saab Zero Defect – nobody explained it to me that way!" It's simple.

33

Teach Him...

Be a buddy to your children – don't be just a parent, be a friend! Hold their hands when they need comforting, but when needed, nudge them in the right direction.

"...He will have to learn. I know that all men are not just, all men are not true.

Teach him that for every scoundrel there is a hero; that for every selfish politician, there is a dedicated leader.

Teach him that for every enemy there is a friend. It will take them, I know, but teach him, if you can, that a dollar earned is of far more value than five pound.

Teach him to learn to lose and also to enjoy winning. Steer him away from envy, if you can, teach him the secret of quiet laughter. Let him learn early that bullies are the easiest to lick.

Teach him, if you can, the wonder of books but also give him quite some time to ponder the eternal mystery of birds in the sky, bees in the sun, and flowers on the green hillside.

In school, teach him that it is far more honorable to fail than to cheat.

Teach him to have faith in his own ideas, even if everyone tells him they are wrong.

Teach him to be gentle with gentle people, and tough with tough. Try to give him the strength not to follow the crowd when everyone is getting on the bandwagon.

Teach him to listen to all men but teach him also to filter all he hears on a screen of truth and take only the good that comes through.

Teach him, if you can, how to laugh when he is sad.

Teach him there is no shame in tears.

Teach him to scoff at cynics and beware of too much sweetness.

Teach him to sell his brawn and brain to the highest bidders, but never to put a price tag on his heart and soul.

Teach him to close his ears to the howling mob and to stand up and fight if he thinks he is right.

Teach him gently, but do not cuddle fine steel. Let him have the courage to be impatient; let him have the patience to be brave.

Teach him always to have sublime faith in mankind.

This is a big order, but see what you can do. He is such a fine little fellow, my son."

Abraham Lincoln

34

KFP/BFP (*Kee Farak Painda/ Bahut Farak Painda*)

When we are not engaged in thinking about some definite problem, we usually spend about 95 per cent of our time thinking about ourselves.

On how to handle "Respond, Don't React" situation, I'd like to give you an excellent true story which will, in all probability, stick in your mind.

Coca Cola and Pepsi were having cola war after the launch of Diet Coke in the USA.

Pepsi came out with the concept of the young generation and went in for a record-breaking $5 million contract with Michael Jackson. But for responding, this contract would have been in the courts causing stress to the Pepsi management and its bottlers.

It happened like this. It was stated in the agreement that Jackson's face would be shown 5½ times. When Jackson saw the film rushes, he put his foot down and wanted it not more than 4½ times.

Now, the Pepsi management knew for sure that they had a watertight contract and decided to go to court to teach a lesson to the "brat." As luck would have it, the very young president asked the graying marketing manager for his opinion. He responded "what difference do 5½ or 4½ circles make to our overall objective?"

If ever anyone came to know of our fight over this one circle, they would think that we were a bunch of idiots! The young president agreed!

Your estimation in your own eyes is more important. Other people's comment should be taken only objectively as an opportunity to re-examine yourself and take corrective action as required.

35

Perfection is Not Always Paralysis!

Happy employees, not TQM or reengineering, hold the key to the future productivity and company success.

An executive from one of the major airlines boarded one of his own aircraft route to a business meeting. Before they left the gate, the executive pulled down the tray table from the seat in front of him and found a coffee stain on it. He refused to let the plane leave until the flight attendants had gone through and checked every tray table on the entire aircraft. The crew quickly went through the cabin, did a few spot cleanings, and in only a minute or two they were in the air heading towards their destination.

During the flight one of the attendants approached the executive and asked him why he made such a big deal about a little coffee stain on his tray table. His answer was simple. Perception. He asked the flight attendant, "If one of our paying passengers pulls down his table and finds a stain on it, what will his perception of our airlines be?"

The attendant thought for a moment and recognized that the perception would be that the airline does not care or that they don't pay attention to details. Perhaps this would lead a customer to wonder, "How well do they service their engines?" It would have created a loss of confidence in the airlines altogether.

Winners develop the habit of doing the things that losers don't like to do.

36

Be a Do-er, and Not a Dot-er!

My problem was I kept reading books on leadership and excellence and management when I should have been working.

Akbar and Birbal shared a wonderful relationship. Birbal was highly talented, well-mannered, and cultured. Above all he had a "thinking" attitude. His attitude was that he could be fired any day. He was also aware that tomorrow's job depended upon today's performance and not that of yesterday.

Akbar used to ask "stupid" questions, and Birbal had the wit and patience to request a day, a week, or a month to come back with the answer – the attitude of suspended conclusion. A very wise thing to do.

Once, on being asked by Akbar, Birbal painted the emperor's portrait in six days. Akbar asked his courtiers to comment on the portrait. Each one put a dot on the portrait wherever he felt it was not good.

Akbar asked Birbal to explain. Birbal thought and called for blank canvases for his colleagues and asked them to do the portrait.

No one came forward. Akbar, with drooping eyes, murmured, "Dot-ers."

Moral: It is easy to find faults in what others do, but difficult to do it yourself.

Excellence in action in an organisation is when employees: pay attention to details, do things right the first time, and practice good human relations.

37

Give Specific Instructions

Everybody, Somebody, Anybody, Nobody

The best way to
get things done
is to allow your
subordinates to
formulate their own
methods of operation.

This is a story about four people named, Everybody, Somebody, Anybody and Nobody. There was an important job to be done and Everybody was sure that Somebody would do it. Anybody could have done it but Nobody did it. Somebody got angry about that because it was Everybody's job. Everybody thought Anybody could do it but Nobody realised that Everybody wouldn't do it. It ended up that Everybody blamed Somebody when Nobody did what Anybody could have done!